S0-BUW-019

In loving memory of my father   A.J.
Dedicated with love to Bori, Lenke,
and Andris   K.K.N.

Text by Antonia Jackson
Illustrations copyright © 2013 Krisztina Kállai Nagy
This edition copyright © 2013 Lion Hudson

The right of Krisztina Kallai Nagy to be identified as the illustrator of this
work has been asserted by her in accordance with the Copyright, Designs
and Patents Act 1988.

All rights reserved. No part of this publication may be reproduced or
transmitted in any form or by any means, electronic or mechanical, including
photocopy, recording, or any information storage and retrieval system,
without permission in writing from the publisher.

Published by Lion Children's Books
an imprint of
Lion Hudson plc
Wilkinson House, Jordan Hill Road,
Oxford OX2 8DR, England
www.lionhudson.com/lionchildrens
ISBN 978 0 7459 6392 1

First edition 2013

A catalogue record for this book is available from the British Library

Printed and bound in China, June 2013, LH11

My Advent Calendar
Christmas Book

Antonia Jackson
Illustrated by Krisztina Kállai Nagy

LI🐾N
CHILDREN'S

Mary lived in a town called Nazareth.
"How happy I am," she said to herself.
"I am engaged to be married to Joseph,
and looking forward to our life together."

Just then, an angel appeared.

"Do not be afraid," the angel said. "Good news! God has chosen you to be the mother of his Son. He will be God's chosen king and will grow up to give the world God's blessing."

Mary was surprised, but promised to do as God wanted.

When Joseph found out, he was sad.

"Mary's baby isn't my baby," he sighed. "I will have to break our engagement."

Then an angel spoke to him in a dream.

"Joseph, God wants you to marry Mary. You will take care of his child and name him Jesus."

Joseph promised to do as God wanted.

Joseph went to talk to Mary.

"We must go to my hometown, Bethlehem. The emperor wants everyone to put their names down on a big list.

"I want us to be put down as husband and wife."
They set off for Bethlehem together.

There was no room to stay anywhere in Bethlehem.
The town was full of people needing to put their names
on the emperor's list.

But Mary's baby was soon to be born.
"We can stay in this stable," said Joseph.
"It is safe and warm."

There, as the oxen munched
and the chickens clucked, baby
Jesus was born.

Mary wrapped him in strips
of cloth and laid him in the
manger.

Meanwhile, out on the hillsides, shepherds were looking after their sheep. Suddenly an angel appeared. "Do not be afraid," the angel said. "Good news! God's Son has been born in Bethlehem. He is God's chosen king and will grow up to give the world God's blessing. "You will find him wrapped in cloth and lying in a manger."

The shepherds were astonished. "We must
go to Bethlehem and find out if this is true,"
they said to each other.

They found Mary and Joseph and the baby
Jesus in the stable.

The shepherds told Mary what the angel had said,
and she thought carefully about their every word.

In lands far to the east, three wise men had spotted
a star.

"The scrolls say that this means a king has been
born," they said. "We must go and find him and
give him gifts."

They followed the star to Jerusalem and began
asking questions.

"We have been following a new star: a sign that a king has been born. Where can we find him?"

King Herod was not happy at this news. He demanded to see the men.

"It is said that a great king will one day be born in Bethlehem.

"I would like you to find him. Then come and tell me where he is."

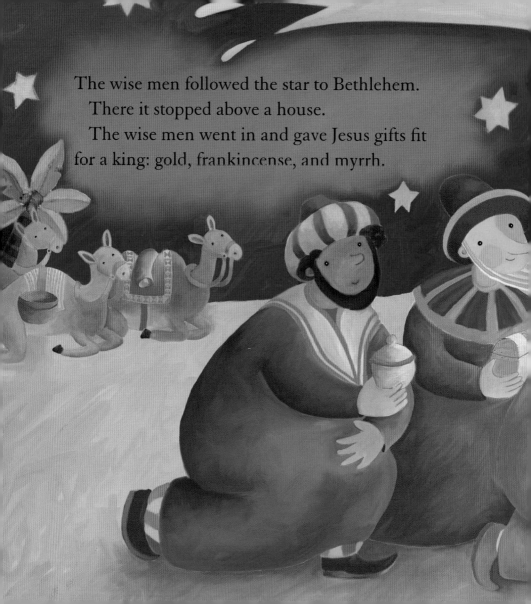

The wise men followed the star to Bethlehem.
There it stopped above a house.
The wise men went in and gave Jesus gifts fit
for a king: gold, frankincense, and myrrh.

Then an angel spoke to the wise men in a dream.
"You must not go back to Herod. He is looking for
the baby and wants to harm him."

The wise men went home by a different road.

An angel also warned Joseph about Herod in a
dream and told him to take his family to Egypt.

"We must leave now," he told Mary.

They left and kept Jesus safe, so that he could grow up to give the world God's blessing.